JEFFREY AND
THE THIRD-GRADE GHOST

# Mysterious Max

Other *Jeffrey and the Third-Grade Ghost* Books

# Jeffrey and the Third-Grade Ghost

## BOOK ONE

# Mysterious Max

### Megan Stine
AND
### H. William Stine

FAWCETT COLUMBINE
NEW YORK

RLI: $\dfrac{\text{VL2 + up}}{\text{IL3 + up}}$

A Fawcett Columbine Book
Published by Ballantine Books
Copyright © 1988 by Cloverdale Press, Inc.

Library of Congress Catalog Card Number: 88-91959

ISBN: 0-449-90326-5
Text design by Mary A. Wirth
Illustrations by Keith Birdsong
Manufactured in the United States of America
First Edition: November 1988
10  9  8  7  6  5  4  3  2  1

To Ellen Steiber
with much appreciation for
her clarity, perception, and
gentle editorial touch.

JEFFREY AND
THE THIRD-GRADE GHOST

# Mysterious Max

# Chapter One

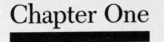

Jeffrey Becker and his third-grade teacher, Mrs. Merrin, got off on the wrong foot the very first day of school. It happened while Mrs. Merrin was reading a story to the red reading group. The blue group was supposed to be working on a math sheet. Jeffrey was in the blue group.

Suddenly, Mrs. Merrin stopped reading.

"Jeffrey Becker," said the pretty, young teacher in a stern voice, "did you just throw the globe across the room?"

Everyone in the class looked at Jeffrey. Their looks seemed to say, "Okay, Jeffrey. Let's see you talk your way out of this one."

"No, Mrs. Merrin," Jeffrey said. "I didn't *throw* the globe. It slipped out of my hands, probably because I was looking at the country of *Greece*."

Everyone in the class except Mrs. Merrin laughed. She just pushed her round, red reading glasses onto her forehead and looked at Jeffrey.

"Jeffrey Becker, you have a detention," she said.

"A *detention*?" Jeffrey said. "No one gives a detention on the first day of school. I think there's a law against it. You could get up to three years in jail with no french fries."

"Make that two detentions," Mrs. Merrin said.

That's how Jeffrey earned detentions for the first *and* second days of school.

On the third day of school, Jeffrey had another detention. This time it was for not bringing his summer-reading book report to class.

When it was Jeffrey's turn to give his book report, he stood up. He brushed his straight brown hair out of his freckled face. Then he pulled two carrots and an avocado out of his backpack. "Uh-oh. My mom must have gotten confused," Jeffrey said. "She put this stuff in my backpack and my book report in the juicer!"

After school that day, Mrs. Merrin told Jeffrey to think about all of the wild stories he told. So Jeffrey thought about them. He thought Mrs. Merrin should have believed him. After all, they were good stories.

On the fourth day of school, Jeffrey got a detention for hitting Arvin Pubbler on the back with an apple-butter-and-jelly sandwich.

"But, Mrs. Merrin," Jeffrey explained. "Didn't

you see it? There was a deadly spider crawling on Arvin's back! I just saved his life."

Mrs. Merrin didn't see it, but she did see Jeffrey after school for the fourth day in a row.

Jeffrey sat at his desk and Mrs. Merrin sat at hers. They didn't speak to each other. Jeffrey was supposed to be writing twenty-five reasons for not lying. But Jeffrey didn't think the punishment was fair. As far as he was concerned, he didn't tell lies. He just made up funny stories to make life more interesting.

Mrs. Merrin straightened up the classroom and wrote things in her teacher's notebook. Then she took two photos out of her purse and looked from one to the other.

Finally, she said to Jeffrey, "My husband and I want to buy a dog. But we can't decide which kind."

"Dogs love me," Jeffrey said. "They can read my mind. They do what I want before I even tell them."

The teacher shook her short blond hair. "Jeffrey, that's absurd," she said.

"It's the *truth*," Jeffrey said sincerely.

"Jeffrey, have you ever heard of the boy who cried wolf?"

"Did he get a lot of detentions, too?" Jeffrey asked.

"He lied so much that no one believed him when he told the truth," Mrs. Merrin said. She put her photos away and stood up. "I'm going to the office. You work on your list—and your attitude."

The moment she left, Jeffrey went to work on his list. First, he added a fancy red border with a crayon. Then he used markers to draw a baseball glove in the corner. After all, how could a list be complete without a drawing of a baseball glove?

"Jeffrey!" a voice outside called to him. It was Benjamin Hyde, Jeffrey's best friend. He was waiting for Jeffrey on the playground.

Jeffrey ran to the window and climbed onto a desk to look out. Benjamin was two stories down. He waved up at the third-grade classroom window. Ben had curly brown hair and gold, wire-rimmed glasses. His glasses seemed to glow in the sunlight.

Ben and Jeffrey had been best friends ever since kindergarten, when the class was studying dinosaurs. One day the teacher had called on Jeffrey to explain why dinosaurs became extinct. Jeffrey, as usual, had been ready with a smart answer.

"Mrs. Gorshlak, dinosaurs aren't extinct," he had explained. "They just went to another planet where no one could make fun of them for being so ugly."

Ben had laughed. Even in kindergarten Ben

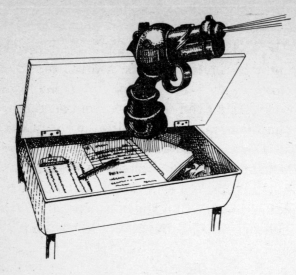

had known more than anyone else about dinosaurs. He had thought Jeffrey's answer was great—unscientific, unbelievable, but great. They had been best friends from then on.

"Come on down, Jeffrey," another voice called. It was Melissa McKane. She was standing next to Ben.

Melissa McKane was Jeffrey's next-door neighbor. She was so much taller than Ben that she practically made a shadow on him. Melissa's hair was long and red. And she always wore it in a ponytail to keep it out of her face in case she suddenly decided to climb a tree, walk all the way home on her hands, or pitch nine innings of baseball. And she did all of those things superbly.

"Hey, Jeffrey," Ben shouted. He pulled out a small plastic squirt gun and aimed it up at the window. "Say 'ah.'"

Jeffrey saw the tiny squirt gun and laughed. It looked like an ordinary, dumb squirt gun, the kind that leaks faster than it shoots. Jeffrey knew that Ben was too far away to hit a target two stories above the ground.

"Ready, aim, fire!" Melissa shouted.

Ben squeezed the trigger. And suddenly a blast of water hit Jeffrey smack in the face. One second Jeffrey was laughing at Ben. The next second he was soaking wet.

"What do you think?" Ben asked with a wicked grin. "I've been working on it in my laboratory." Ben wanted to be a mad scientist when he grew up. He called his bedroom his laboratory.

"Uh . . . pretty cool," Jeffrey called out. Then he turned around quickly and glanced at the door. Mrs. Merrin still hadn't come back.

"But not as cool as the Super Power Water Blaster than I've got hidden under my notebook," Jeffrey muttered to himself. He ran back to his desk, water still dripping from his face.

He opened his desktop, started to reach in— and snatched his hand back. His muscles froze, his mouth dropped open, and he forgot how to breathe.

There, floating in midair inside of his desk, was *a living hand*! It wasn't connected to an arm or a body, or to anything else for that matter. It was just a hand floating inside Jeffrey's desk.

Before Jeffrey even had time to slam the desk-top shut, the hand picked up his Super Power Water Blaster and squirted him in the face.

"I don't believe this," Jeffrey said. "I just got squirted with my own gun!"

# Chapter Two

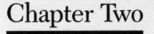

Jeffrey couldn't move. He looked and felt like a statue. If the statue had a title, it would be, "Boy Frozen at His Desk with His Mouth Open Wide Enough for Birds to Nest In." Did what just happened really happen? Did a ghostly hand actually squirt him in the face with his own gun? Or did he just think it happened?

There was only one way to find out: He had to look in his desk again. But just as Jeffrey was about to peek in, Mrs. Merrin came back into the classroom. Jeffrey closed his desk with a slam that made Mrs. Merrin jump. She looked at Jeffrey carefully.

"What's going on?" she asked.

"You wouldn't believe me if I told you," Jeffrey said.

"It's worth a try, isn't it?" the teacher asked with a smile.

"I've been working on my list, that's all," Jeffrey said.

"You're right. It doesn't fly, Jeffrey," Mrs. Merrin said in a calm voice. "Why is your face soaking wet?"

"I'm sweating. It's really hot in here, don't you think?"

Mrs. Merrin shook her head. With a sigh, she walked toward Jeffrey.

She was going to look in his desk—Jeffrey knew it. He wanted to stop her, but he didn't know how.

When Mrs. Merrin pulled open the desk lid, Jeffrey held his breath. Finally, he looked down. His books were there. His notebooks were there. His squirt gun was there. But the hand was gone!

Mrs. Merrin kept the squirt gun and picked up the list Jeffrey had been writing.

### 25 REASONS NOT TO LIE
#### by Jeffrey Becker

1. It gets you into trouble with your teacher.
2. It sets a bad example for pets.
3. In certain people, it makes your nose grow.
4. TV commercials do it better.
5–15. These reasons are too embarrassing to be talked about in public.
16–25. These reasons are rated R and I'm too young to know about them.

"A true masterpiece," Mrs. Merrin said. But she was laughing when she said it. She walked back to her desk and started washing the blackboard with Jeffrey's squirt gun. "I'm going to think about you a lot tonight, Jeffrey," she said. "And tomorrow things are going to be different in this class."

"Things are different right now," Jeffrey said, taking a quick peek in his desk. But the hand was still gone.

When detention was over, Jeffrey left the school building. Melissa and Ben were still waiting outside for him.

"Listen," Melissa said. "Who knows what extremely important event is coming up in four weeks?"

Jeffrey was only half listening. His mind was still on the hand in his desk. But Ben immediately began to guess.

"The World Series?" Ben said. "Your brother, Gary, takes his once-a-month bath?"

Melissa shook her head so much she looked like a windshield wiper. "No, Ben. I'll give you a hint. Someone terrific is having a birthday."

"My birthday isn't until January," Ben said.

"Not *you!*" Melissa said. "Me! And I'm officially inviting you and Jeffrey to my party."

"Does this mean your brother *isn't* going to take a bath?" Ben teased.

"Leave Gary out of this," Melissa said. "*I* certainly plan to. Now here's the deal. I'm going to have a rock-'n'-roll party in my backyard. But I need some help setting everything up. Would you give me a hand, Jeffrey?"

Suddenly, Jeffrey was paying attention. "A *hand*?" he gasped.

"You don't have to help if you don't want to," Melissa said. She sounded a little hurt.

"Uh, sure I'll help, Melissa," Jeffrey said. "But that's four weeks away!"

"I like to be organized," Melissa said.

By this time they were standing in front of Jeffrey's house. Ben sat down on the curb. It was almost dinnertime. But Ben would do anything to avoid going home after school. That's when he was supposed to take out his family's trash.

"How about some football?" Ben asked.

"Can't," Melissa said. "My mom and dad are going out tonight. I've got to get home so I can talk to the baby-sitter before Gary does."

"Why?" Jeffrey asked.

"Because the last time my parents went out, it was awful. Gary told the baby-sitter I was being punished. The big creep convinced her I wasn't allowed to have anything to eat the whole night—or to watch TV!"

"Well, we all know what's waiting for me at home: the trash." Ben groaned. "The kitchen trash and the bathroom trash and the bedroom trash. And I've got to take it all out. You know, someday I'm going to invent an animal that will eat all the trash in the house—or maybe you could just send your brother over, Melissa."

"I heard that," shouted Gary McKane. Melissa's brother had been spying on them from behind a tree. He ran out and grabbed Ben's book bag off his shoulder. "Got anything in here I need?" Gary asked, unzipping the bag. As usual, Gary was picking on Melissa's friends.

"Hey! Give that back," Ben said. "Just because you're in the fifth grade doesn't mean you're *required* to be obnoxious."

Gary snarled. Gary always snarled when Ben used a word he didn't understand. But he didn't give back Ben's bag.

Jeffrey decided to try to help—in a sneaky way.

"Come on, Ben," Jeffrey said. "You *know* what's in your book bag. Let him look." Jeffrey pretended to hide a smile. "Go on and look, Gary."

Gary stopped and stared at Jeffrey.

"What's so funny, Becker? Why do you want me to look in the bag? What's in there?"

"Nothing," Jeffrey said, almost laughing. "Go on, Gary."

Gary threw the bag at Jeffrey. "I'm not putting my hand in there—*you* are, Becker. Let's see you do it."

Jeffrey reached slowly into Ben's bag. Then he quickly pulled out Ben's power-laser squirt gun. With one squeeze of the trigger, he almost drowned Gary.

"Now you won't have to wait four weeks for a bath!" Jeffrey shouted at Gary. Melissa and Ben fell on the ground, laughing. Jeffrey laughed, too, but he ran full speed into his own house.

"Hi, Mom. I'm home," Jeffrey said, locking the door behind him.

Jeffrey's mother was sitting at the family computer, writing a newsletter for the school P.T.A. "Mrs. Merrin called," she said.

"She did?" Jeffrey asked with a king-sized gulp.

"She called to say you forgot your squirt gun," Jeffrey's mother said. "She put it inside your desk. It will be waiting for you in the morning."

"She did?" Jeffrey said. "Oh, that's great."

But as he walked up to his room, he thought to himself, I wonder what else will be waiting for me in my desk tomorrow. He decided to get there bright and early to find out.

He hoped it would be the mysterious, living hand!

# Chapter Three

The next morning Jeffrey woke up before anyone else in his house. He was already eating his breakfast when his father came into the kitchen—and *that* was early! Jeffrey's father was an electrical engineer. He had to get up early every morning to go to his job at a construction site.

"Are you up early or am I in the wrong house?" asked Mr. Becker.

"Gotta be at school first thing, Dad," Jeffrey said. "I'm trying out a new program."

"What is it? French? Computers? Woodworking?"

"It's called sunrise detention," Jeffrey lied. "It's for kids who don't want to waste a minute of daylight."

Mr. Becker blinked once. "I'm sure you'll do fine," he said. "You caught on to the afternoon detention like a pro."

Jeffrey got to school even before Mrs. Merrin.

When he tried the doorknob, the classroom was locked. He stared into the room through the window, trying to see if there was anything strange around his desk.

Soon, he saw Mrs. Merrin walking down the hall. "Well, this is a surprise, Jeffrey," she said. "A pleasant surprise. Let's have a talk."

"Sure," Jeffrey said, putting his hand on the doorknob. He waited for Mrs. Merrin to unlock the door.

"How about outside?" Mrs. Merrin said.

"Outside?" Jeffrey asked, staring into the classroom again.

"Sure," his pretty teacher said. "It's fall. The leaves are fading and so is my hay fever. So let's get some fresh air."

"Fresh air? Did you know that Denver has some of the highest air pollution in the country?" Jeffrey said.

"I know, Jeffrey. But we live a thousand miles from Denver," said Mrs. Merrin. "Let's risk it."

Reluctantly, Jeffrey followed his teacher outside.

"I told you I'd think about you last night and I did—in between trying to decide with my husband which dog we want to buy," Mrs. Merrin said. She picked up red and yellow leaves as they walked. "I have a new attitude today and some good news. I'm not going to give you any more detentions."

No detentions? Jeffrey wondered if they had invented a new punishment overnight. He always knew grown-ups did sneaky things after kids went to bed.

"You aren't allowed to beat me, you know," Jeffrey said.

Mrs. Merrin put a leaf on Jeffrey's head and smiled. "I don't think you need detentions. I think you need to get the class's attention some other way—not by making up stories."

It was time to walk back to the classroom. Mrs. Merrin was all smiles. As soon as she unlocked the door, Jeffrey rushed to his desk. He swung the lid open. Inside lay his squirt gun with a note. "Thanks for the loan. Mrs. M." He searched under everything—but there was no hand.

I didn't dream it. I know I didn't dream it, Jeffrey thought.

The classroom was filling up, but Jeffrey wished he were all alone.

Hey! Maybe that was it. The hand appeared yesterday when Jeffrey was alone in the classroom. How could he be alone again?

There was only one way, he decided. Another detention! He had to get another detention. But it wasn't going to be easy. Mrs. Merrin had picked today to think up a ridiculous idea like not giving any detentions.

Jeffrey leaned over to Ben, who was reading a book called *Ten Science Experiments That Might Blow Up Your House*.

"Bet your lunch I can get a detention without saying a single word," Jeffrey said.

"You're on," Ben said. "But I'm warning you. My mom gave me turkey bologna today."

"That's okay," Jeffrey said. As long as I get a detention, I'll eat anything, he thought to himself.

Jeffrey opened his desktop, took out his water gun, and aimed at Arvin's back.

Mrs. Merrin looked calmly at Jeffrey. "I knew you would test me, Jeffrey. No detention, but I'll take the gun again. Now behave yourself."

Later, during arts and crafts, Jeffrey whispered to Melissa that Mrs. Merrin had accidentally lost her wedding ring in one of the paint jars. Then he sat back and watched the action. Jeffrey knew there was no better way to get anything organized than by telling Melissa. Soon she had most of the class stuffing their hands into paint jars, spilling and splashing paint. It made a truly memorable mess.

"Jeffrey, clean all of this up right now," Mrs. Merrin said.

"And see you after school?" Jeffrey asked, trying to finish her sentence.

"No detention," Mrs. Merrin said.

After noon recess, Jeffrey was getting desperate. So he came into the classroom without his shirt on. He said he wanted to give a book report on "The Emperor's New Clothes."

"Jeffrey Becker!" Mrs Merrin said. Her voice was no longer calm. "Are you *trying* to get another detention?"

"Yes," Jeffrey said.

"Why? Tell us all why this is so important to you."

"You want the truth?" Jeffrey asked.

"The absolute truth," Mrs. Merrin said.

"All right," Jeffrey answered. "This is the absolute truth. Yesterday I saw a living hand floating inside my desk. And I want to stay after school to see if it's still there today."

Mrs. Merrin threw her hands up in the air. "That does it. You have a detention for lying."

Jeffrey was happy for the rest of the day, although he didn't feel great about the way Mrs. Merrin looked at him. She wasn't angry. She just seemed sad.

After school, Jeffrey sat behind his desk and Mrs. Merrin sat behind hers.

"See your living hand yet?" she asked without looking up at him.

"I think I have to be alone to see it," Jeffrey said.

Mrs. Merrin stood up. "My husband was going to take off work early today," she said. "We were going to go to the pet store to buy our new dog. Now we can't." Then she left the room.

As soon as she left, Jeffrey opened his desk.

It was there!

It was a hand, a hand about as big as Jeffrey's. It was floating inside his desk! Slowly, it floated up into

21

the space above his desk. Then it swooped around Jeffrey once.

Jeffrey's heart was pounding. He was almost afraid to move.

A minute later, the hand began to grow, or rather to fill in. First, an arm appeared. Then another hand and another arm. Then Jeffrey saw a chest materialize. It was wearing a plaid flannel shirt. Then two legs in baggy blue jeans with cuffs appeared. Little by little, a transparent boy was taking shape right before Jeffrey's eyes!

It was a boy about Jeffrey's age. He had black hair slicked back on the sides. Somehow he had gotten Jeffrey's water gun back from Mrs. Merrin. He was twirling it around his finger the way a cowboy would. And he floated in midair!

There were lots of things to say about what was happening. But Jeffrey summed it up in three words.

"You're a ghost!" he cried.

# Chapter Four

Jeffrey stood up fast, knocking his chair over behind him. His feet couldn't move, but his mind was racing as he stared at the ghost. What was he doing here? What did he want?

Then the ghost smiled a sly smile and started to open his mouth. Jeffrey held his breath. The ghost was going to speak to him.

The ghost stopped twirling the water gun and said, "Like, what's shaking, Daddy-o?"

What did that mean? The only things shaking were Jeffrey's knees. And did the ghost really think Jeffrey was his father? "Do you speak English?" Jeffrey asked cautiously.

"Don't be so squaresville," said the ghost. "And wipe that are-you-really-a-ghost? look off your face. What do I look like? A slice of pizza? Stay cool, Jeffrey."

Jeffrey backed away a step. "How do you know my name?" he said.

"Are you putting me on? I've been watching you

all week. Man, when you threw the globe across the room, that cracked me up, Daddy-o," said the ghost.

"Yeah, I thought that was pretty good, too," Jeffrey said, relaxing for a second. "I can't believe this. I'm talking to a ghost."

The ghost grinned. "I haven't had anyone to talk to for years."

"What's your name?" Jeffrey asked.

"My friends used to call me Max," the ghost answered. "But my mom called me Maxwell. And my dad called me 'Didn't I tell you not to read comic books at the dinner table?'"

Jeffrey laughed and Max laughed even louder. He flew over and started walking on top of Mrs. Merrin's desk.

"This used to be my school before they closed it down," Max said. "Now it's all painted, with weird new lights and stuff. They even gave it a new name—Redwood School. When I went here, it was called Bragaw School," the ghost went on. "And I was the coolest kid in the third grade. We stole the room keys all the time. Once we even stole the piano keys."

A ghost talking to you nonstop was strange enough. But even stranger—Max was talking to Jeffrey like a friend.

24

Max shook his head. "This place just doesn't look like it did in '55."

"Wow! Is that the year you . . ." Jeffrey stopped. He didn't want to say anything that would hurt Max's feelings.

"The year I graduated to ghostville?" Max said. "Yeah, Daddy-o."

"What happened?" Jeffrey asked. But he wasn't sure he really wanted to know.

"Detentions," Max answered. "I had the longest detentions of anybody. Like, by the time I got out of school every day, my teacher grew a beard. And that was Mrs. Scott. Yeah, that's what happened. I was in detention so long, everyone just forgot about me."

Max looked at Jeffrey and Jeffrey knew that look. Max was checking to see if Jeffrey believed his story or not.

"Hey, you don't believe me?" Max said. "Like, if I'm lying, I'm flying."

Jeffrey looked at the ghost's feet, which were floating two feet off the ground. "You *are* flying, Max," Jeffrey said. "Boy, if I were a ghost, there are a million things I'd do. I'd glue the teacher's grade books closed. And I'd put plaster of paris in the finger paint—"

"Who do you think invented the 'teacher lost

her wedding ring in the paint jars' trick?" Max said. "I did! But after twenty or thirty years, it starts to get lonely. Ghosts have to be careful about talking to people. Say hi to the wrong person and it's heart-attack city. Next thing you know, you've got a new ghost buddy. You're the first cat I thought it would be safe to talk to."

That made Jeffrey smile. But he couldn't help adding, "And safe to squirt in the face!"

"I did not. I was just trying to see how your gun worked and your face got in the way," Max explained. "But when I saw you in detention day after day, and I heard the stories you made up, I knew you were my kind of guy."

Just then the classroom door began to open. "Uh-oh. See you later, alligator," Max said. And then he was gone. Like a window shade rolling up, he disappeared into thin air.

"Jeffrey? Are you all right?" Mrs. Merrin asked. She was standing in the doorway with a concerned look on her face. "You're white as a sheet."

"They don't wear sheets. They wear plaid flannel shirts," Jeffrey said.

"Jeffrey, you're not making much sense. Did you eat a well-balanced lunch?" asked Mrs. Merrin, walking to her desk.

"Turkey bologna," Jeffrey answered. He hadn't

gotten the detention until after lunch, but Ben gave him his sandwich anyway.

"Oh. Well, did you see your hand?" she asked.

Jeffrey didn't want to answer. "Uh, can I go now?" he asked.

"I'm ready to go home if you are," said the teacher. "Maybe you can write *me* an excuse, telling my husband why I'm late."

Jeffrey stopped by her desk and watched her fill her briefcase. "I'm sorry you didn't buy your puppy today," he said.

Mrs. Merrin smiled her Mrs. Merrin smile, not her teacher smile. "Thanks," she said.

"See you later, alligator," Jeffrey shouted on his way out the door.

"After a while, crocodile," Mrs. Merrin called after him.

Jeffrey stopped, turned to Mrs. Merrin, and looked around the empty classroom. "Hey, thanks. I'll have to remember that one," he said.

# Chapter Five

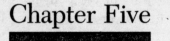

Jeffrey closed Mrs. Merrin's door behind him. "Max," he whispered into the empty hall. "Are you here?"

His voice echoed and disappeared. There was no one there. Jeffrey waited until he was sure of that.

Only the squeak of his own sneakers followed Jeffrey down the hall and out the door. He squinted into the late-afternoon sun as he walked down the steps of the school.

"Like, what took you so long?"

Max was standing by the flagpole—and he wasn't transparent anymore! He looked as real as Jeffrey and as happy to see him, too.

"This is great!" Jeffrey said, pulling Max by the arm. "This is perfect. Come on. We've got to hurry."

"Hey, don't bruise the merchandise. Where are we going?"

"To a baseball game."

"Baseball!" Max laughed. "That's just what I'm ready for."

"All my friends are there," Jeffrey said. "I can't wait for them to meet you."

Max grinned but didn't say anything.

On the way to the park, Jeffrey told Max about his team. They were called the Beefrolls because a store named Beefroll Bob's was supposed to get them uniforms.

And Max, of course, talked about his favorite subject—himself. "The longest baseball game I ever pitched started on July sixteenth. It lasted so long that we finally had to quit because the snow got too deep to play in."

"Yeah, right. Well, we've already got a pitcher. Her name is Melissa," Jeffrey said as they got to the baseball field.

"Hold the phone!" Max interrupted. "Melissa is a girl's name! You let a *girl* play on your team?"

Jeffrey smiled. Max still didn't realize this was the 1980s. "Melissa can hit farther, run faster, and throw harder than every guy on the team except for Ricky Reyes. What would *you* do with a girl like that, Max?"

Max rubbed his chin and thought for a minute. "Like, I'd make her captain," he said.

"That's just what we did," Jeffrey said. "Listen, Max, there's one thing you've got to be ready for. They may not believe me at first about you being a ghost. My friends sort of think that sometimes I make stories up."

"If they can tell, you must not be making up good ones," Max said with a sly smile.

Jeffrey rolled his eyes and ran over to the bench where the Beefrolls were sitting. The game had already started. Ricky Reyes was at bat. The other team was on the field. Max followed right behind Jeffrey.

"Hey, you guys, I want you to meet Max," Jeffrey said.

"Sure, we'll meet him anytime," Melissa said. "Kenny, get ready. You're up after Ricky."

Kenny Thompsen was a short, shy kid. He wore his blond hair in an overgrown crewcut. He put down the book he was reading and stood up.

"Jeffrey, you're late!" scolded Captain Melissa. "Why did you get a detention on purpose today? You *know* we're playing the Lions. They're the toughest team in the Little League."

"Max can explain that," Jeffrey said, winking at his new friend.

"Yeah, when he gets here," said Benjamin Hyde.

"What do you mean 'when he gets here'?" Jeffrey asked. "He's right here. This is Max."

Max slicked his hair back with his hand and smiled at Jeffrey.

"What are you talking about, Jeffrey? There's nobody there," Melissa said. "And we don't have time for any stories."

There was the smack of a bat against a baseball and the crowd went wild. Ricky Reyes, the heavy hitter on Jeffrey's team, had just hit a home run.

"Come on, you guys, stop fooling around," Jeffrey said with a nervous laugh. "I told Max he could be on our team."

"Fine. When he gets here, he can be on the team," Melissa said.

"He *is* here!" Jeffrey shouted. He didn't know why his friends were playing this stupid game, but he wanted them to stop. "Max, say something."

"Bad scene, Daddy-o. I forgot to tell you I'm invisible to everyone but you," Max said with a laugh.

"Oh, no." Jeffrey moaned. "You mean that only I can see and hear you?" Jeffrey turned back to his friends. "Listen, you guys aren't going to believe this."

"That's nothing new," Ben said.

Jeffrey tried to explain it in his calmest voice.

"There's a ghost in my desk at school. His name is Max. And he came to the game with me. He's standing right here, but I'm the only one who can see him. You guys believe me, don't you?"

"Sure we believe you," Ben said. "Aren't you the same guy who said you were teaching penguins how to speak French?"

"Yeah, and aren't you the same guy who told us when your mom cooked liver, it tasted just like chocolate pudding?" asked Kenny.

"Yuck—I haven't been able to eat chocolate pudding ever since," Melissa said.

"Okay, okay, I get the picture," Jeffrey said. "But you guys are wrong. Max is here."

"Can we play some baseball?" Ben said.

The game continued and the Beefrolls played their best. But it wasn't enough. The Lions were too tough. At the top of the ninth inning, the score was Lions, 11, and the Beefrolls, 10. This was the Beefrolls' last chance.

But Jeffrey could hardly keep his mind on the game. He was sitting on the bench and Max was sitting next to him. "I can see you," he said. "Why can't they? They're my best friends."

"That's for me to know and for you to cool out," Max said.

"Jeffrey, you're up next," Melissa called. "Unless *Max* is pinch-hitting."

Jeffrey walked to the plate with his bat and faced the Lion's pitcher for the last time. The pitcher looked big and mean. He had to be in the sixth grade at least.

Before Jeffrey even had his bat ready, the first ball went flying past him.

"Strike one!"

The next pitch went by so fast it hurt the catcher's hand.

"Strike two!"

"But who's counting?" Jeffrey said, trying to joke. He looked at second base. There was Kenny Thompsen, waiting. If Kenny could get to home plate, the game would be tied.

Jeffrey looked back at the pitcher and he couldn't believe what he saw. There was Max standing right behind the pitcher! Max had a beat-up, old baseball glove on. But, of course, only Jeffrey could see him. As the pitcher went into his windup, Max gave him a small shove. The ball came toward Jeffrey as slowly as a paper airplane. And when Jeffrey swung his bat, he connected.

It was a line drive toward third base. Jeffrey ran to first, and the third baseman sprang to catch the ball. Except Max was right there. He stuck his foot out and tripped the third baseman. Then Max picked up the ball and threw it into the outfield.

By the time the Lions pulled themselves together, Kenny and Jeffrey had both reached home plate. And Jeffrey had scored the go-ahead run!

But the next three Beefroll batters struck out. Then the Lions came up to bat. Soon the Lions had two runners on base.

"Well, Jeffrey," Max said, walking up to Jeffrey in right field. "It's been a blast. But it couldn't last."

"What does that mean?" Jeffrey asked.

"See ya later, alligator." Max tossed his glove to Jeffrey.

The leather glove was grimy and soft in all the right places. Someone had broken it in. There were names written on the glove in different colored inks. Duke Snider. Willie Mays. Pee Wee Reese. Roy Campanella. Real autographs from some of the all-time greatest baseball players! "Hey, where did you get this glove, Max?" Jeffrey asked. But when he looked up, Max was gone.

Crack! Another fly ball. It sounded like a home run. It looked like a home run. Jeffrey watched it and knew it was going to sail over his head. And if it did, the Lions would win the ball game.

Jeffrey took off, running as fast as he could. He

knew he didn't have a chance, but he stretched out his left hand, the hand with the glove on it. Suddenly, the glove seemed to lift him off the ground. It carried him like a missile toward the flying baseball. The next thing Jeffrey knew, he was on the ground and the baseball was in his glove!

The game was over and the Beefrolls had won! The whole team crowded around Jeffrey, who was sitting on the ground. They gave each other high-fives and pounded Jeffrey on the back.

"How did you do that?" Melissa asked.

"I didn't," Jeffrey said, still in shock. "The glove did."

Kenny looked at the old glove carefully. "Whose glove is it, anyway?" he asked.

"Max's," Jeffrey said.

"Okay, okay, it's Max's," said Ben, rolling his eyes in disbelief. "So why don't you give it back to him now?"

"I can't. He's gone."

"Well, when are you going to see him again?" asked Melissa.

"I don't know," Jeffrey said. "Maybe he'll be right back."

"Right." Ricky Reyes smiled. "But I'm not waiting around."

"Come on, Jeffrey," Ben said, seeing everyone

leave. "We're all going to my house for a winners' party. Then everyone's going to help me take out the trash."

"In a minute," Jeffrey said.

The winning Beefrolls packed up their stuff and left the field. But Jeffrey stayed back. Standing by himself, he looked up and down the empty field. He was hoping to see Max. Suddenly, he got a feeling that he didn't like. Maybe this time Max wouldn't be right back. Maybe not even for a long time.

Jeffrey kicked the dirt. It was bad enough that no one believed he had met a real ghost. But now Max had disappeared.

What if Max was gone for good?

# Chapter Six

The number of days since Max had disappeared was adding up. Three, seven, ten—then two weeks! Every day Jeffrey woke up hoping that he'd see his friend again. And every day he was disappointed. No Max in his desk at school. No Max on the playground. After the third day, Jeffrey stopped opening his desk fifty times an hour. But he didn't stop hoping.

Finally, one morning, Jeffrey got out of bed and found a surprise. His bedroom slippers were walking around the room all by themselves!

"Max!" Jeffrey shouted.

Slowly, feet appeared in the walking slippers. Then, all of a sudden, Max showed up. He was wearing a new plaid shirt and a new pair of jeans.

"This house is a groove," said the ghost. "You've even got a TV set in the kitchen. I dig all the buttons on it, but the picture's too small."

"Max, that's not a TV set. That's our microwave oven," Jeffrey said. "Where have you been? I've been looking everywhere for you. And I haven't been able to get a detention for a week."

"Try harder. I used to be able to get a detention without even saying a word," was all that Max would say.

Max dropped in and out for the next couple of days. It drove Jeffrey crazy. Just when he and Max were right in the middle of a game of checkers or a videotape, Max would leave. And the worst part was that he would never say where he had been, where he was going, or when he'd be back.

On Saturday morning, one week before Melissa's birthday party, Max found Jeffrey sitting sadly on his bed.

"What's shaking, Jeffrey?" Max asked.

Jeffrey looked at Max and said just one word: "Shopping." To most people it was a simple, common, ordinary word. But to Jeffrey it was a nightmare. "I have to go shopping with my mom. We're going to get my new winter coat." He shook his head. "Something weird happens to my mom when she tries to buy a coat for me."

What Jeffrey meant was that Mrs. Becker was never satisfied. She shopped and shopped until she found the most perfect winter coat in the entire known universe. It usually meant that Jeffrey had to try on every coat in the store.

"Bad scene," Max said.

"Dragsville." Jeffrey sighed.

"Don't sweat it," Max said. "I'll pick out the coat."

"Great!" Jeffrey said.

But when they got into the store, Jeffrey's heart sank. The heat was on, full blast. Even Max couldn't "cool out" here.

"Hey, Mom. It's one hundred and ninety degrees in here," Jeffrey said. "I think the boiler's on the fritz. We'd better get out before it explodes."

"No dice, Jeffrey," Mrs. Becker said. "Now, let's see. Are you a size ten or a twelve? We'd better try both sizes of every coat, just to be sure."

In record time Jeffrey was trying on heavy coats in the hot store. It was the worst. His mother knelt on the floor to get a good look at him.

"Too short," she said of a beige one. "Wrong color," she said of the Day-Glo orange coat. "Too tight in the shoulders," she said, tossing away a green coat with a furry collar.

But while Mrs. Becker was choosing coats for Jeffrey, Max walked around the store doing his own shopping. "Hey, Jeffrey," Max called, pointing to a coat. "Dig this one!" Max dropped it on top of the coat pile.

It was black leather dotted with silver studs and

with a dozen zippered pockets. Jeffrey put it on.

"Coolsville," said Max.

"Jeffrey, take that off immediately. You look like a snow tire with chains," Mrs. Becker said. "Try the blue one on again."

Jeffrey tried on the blue one again. And then a red one. And a tan one and a ski parka with a removable hood. In between those coats, however, he tried on coats picked out by Max. Every time Mrs. Becker turned her back, Max would hand Jeffrey a cool coat.

By the third leather coat with silver zippers, Mrs. Becker was beginning to get mad.

"I didn't pick that one out," she said, seeing her son in a brown leather bomber jacket. "How did it get in the pile?"

"Tell your mom to buy it," Max said. "It's cooler than cool."

"Take it off," Mrs. Becker said. "It's ridiculous." She handed Jeffrey a coat with a weird hood.

"You look like a rabbit," said Max.

"Well," his mother finally said. "It's between these three coats. Try them on, Jeffrey."

"Again?" Jeffrey said. "Wouldn't it be easier if you just brought an instant camera and took my picture?"

"It would be easier if we were born with fur like

the bears. Then we'd never have to buy coats," Mrs. Becker said. "What about the red one?"

"I *hate* the red one," Jeffrey said.

"Let's see it on you again."

Jeffrey frowned as he tried it on again.

Suddenly, Mrs. Becker's eyes grew large. "I didn't see that before," she said. "There's a big blob of bubble gum on the sleeve! How did that get there?"

Jeffrey looked at Max, who just laughed. Then Max blew a bubble with a new piece of gum.

"Take it off," Mrs. Becker said. "We can't buy it now."

"Gee, that's too bad, Mom," Jeffrey said. And he gave Max a big thank-you smile.

Max was getting antsy. "When I went shopping," he bragged, "I told my old lady exactly which coat *I* wanted to buy. Dig?"

"And what happened?" Jeffrey asked.

Max sighed. "She bought the coat *she* wanted."

In the end, Mrs. Becker bought the coat Jeffrey had tried on first—two hours earlier.

By the time Jeffrey, his mom, and Max left the store, Mrs. Becker was worn out. They walked through the mall, looking for a place to get some ice cream.

Just then, Jeffrey saw Mrs. Merrin. She and her husband were coming out of the pet store. She was carrying a little black puppy.

"Jeffrey!" Mrs. Merrin said. "We did it! We finally decided to get the cocker spaniel. Isn't he adorable?"

The puppy was scared to be out in the world. But he was happy to be in Mrs. Merrin's arms. Suddenly, though, he started barking and barking.

"Uh-oh. Troublesville," Max said quickly. "Animals can see me."

The puppy was barking at Max. He didn't like the ghost one bit.

"Jeffrey," Mrs. Merrin teased, "you said dogs love you. What happened?"

"You wouldn't believe me if I told you," Jeffrey said.

"Try me," Mrs. Merrin said with twinkling eyes.

Jeffrey thought about it for a moment.

"The truth?"

"The truth," Mrs. Merrin said. But she was beginning to grin already.

"Well, I was just shopping for a new winter coat," Jeffrey explained. "And my mother made me try on so many coats with fur collars and fur linings, I think I got fleas! That's why your puppy is barking at me. He doesn't like the fleas."

Mrs. Merrin gave Jeffrey's mom an understanding look.

"Get Jeffrey a flea collar before you send him back to school on Monday," she said to Jeffrey's mom. "I don't need *two* dogs in my life—one is enough!"

Then she and her husband took their new, barking puppy and went home.

# Chapter Seven

The next day was Sunday—less than one week before Melissa's birthday. Melissa rang Jeffrey's doorbell bright and early.

"Hi, Jeffrey," she said. "Can you help me today? I want to see if everything's going to work out okay for my party."

"Sure," Jeffrey said.

Just as they were about to leave, Mrs. Becker walked through the living room. "Hi, Melissa," she said. "Want to see Jeffrey's new coat?"

Melissa looked alarmed. "You went coat shopping yesterday?" she asked softly. "How did it go?"

Jeffrey shook his head. "Don't ask," he whispered. "Just tell my mom you love the coat."

Jeffrey went to the closet for his coat. He opened the door. Suddenly, someone pulled him inside by the arm.

"Max!" Jeffrey said. "What are you doing in here?"

"Like, we need to talk right now," Max said.

46

Then he closed the door. "Heart-to-heart, face-to-face, cat-to-cat."

What could be more embarrassing than standing in a coat closet with the door closed? Jeffrey knew his mother and Melissa were staring at the door. Every time Jeffrey moved his arms, a coat hanger hit him in the face.

"Why wasn't I invited to Melissa's birthday party?" Max asked.

"You've got to be kidding," Jeffrey said.

There was a knock at the door.

"Jeffrey? Did you say something?" his mother called.

"No, Mom. Be right out." Then Jeffrey lowered his voice to talk to Max. "For starters, Melissa doesn't know you exist, Max. And even if she did, she couldn't see you. And nobody knows your address. So how could she possibly send you an invitation?"

"Don't bug me about the details," Max said. "I want an invitation."

Jeffrey could see something on Max's face—even in the dark closet. Max's feelings were hurt, although he was trying not to show it. "Max, there'll be other parties," Jeffrey said. "And you're definitely invited to *my* birthday party."

"Like, I'm hip there will be other parties,

Daddy-o—but not like this one," Max said with a strange laugh. "Like, count on it."

What was that supposed to mean? But Max disappeared before Jeffrey could ask the question. He stepped out of the closet wearing his new coat and a very worried look on his face. Max sounded like a ghost with a plan.

"Totally awesome coat, Mrs. Becker. You did it again," Melissa said.

Good old Melissa. She always came through.

"Thanks, Melissa," said Mrs. Becker. "Jeffrey, why were you in the closet?"

"Uh, I was checking to see if I could put my coat on in the dark, Mom. We're having a big test on it in class this week," Jeffrey said. "Come on, Melissa."

Jeffrey and Melissa went next door to Melissa's house. They headed through the kitchen, turned right at the refrigerator, and bumped smack into danger.

"Hi, slimeballs," the danger said. It was Melissa's older brother, Gary. He was lying on his stomach in the living room, reading the Sunday comics.

"Don't worry, Jeffrey," Melissa said. "My brother's been fed. He won't attack."

"Hey, Melissa," Gary said. "I accidentally put my foot through one of your stereo speakers in the backyard. Hope that doesn't ruin your party."

"You'd better not," Melissa said. She hurried through the house and into the backyard.

Melissa looked at her speakers and took a deep breath. "They're fine," she announced.

They could hear Gary laughing inside the house.

"Okay, here's the problem," Melissa said. "I've got my record player up in my tree house. That will be the disc jockey's booth. And I've set my speakers down here on the deck. But I need help stringing the extension cords and speaker wires. I don't know if they're going to reach." Melissa's father worked at a radio station, so Melissa knew a lot about stereo systems.

Melissa leaned a ladder against an old oak tree. Then the two friends immediately got to work. Jeffrey started stringing the extension cords. They had to stretch from an outlet at the back of the house to Melissa's tree house.

"I'll turn on some music. Tell me if it's too loud," Melissa said.

Jeffrey waited. But the music didn't start. The speakers were silent.

"Too loud!" someone shouted. It was Gary. He had come outside to watch.

"Gary, what did you do up here?" Melissa

49

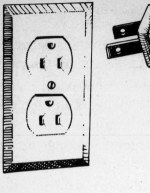
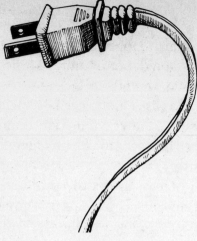

shouted from the tree house. "Nothing works."

"I didn't do anything," Gary said, sipping his soda.

Jeffrey followed the wires from the tree house and quickly discovered the problem. "Melissa," he called, "the cord came out of the wall, that's all." Jeffrey plugged the cord back in.

"Try it again," he shouted to Melissa.

"Still no power," Melissa called back.

Jeffrey looked back at the electrical outlet on the wall of the house. The cord was unplugged again.

"Ha ha haha!" Gary laughed. "He can't even plug in a cord."

Gary laughed himself into the house. He drop-kicked his empty can of soda at Jeffrey as he left.

Jeffrey was angry at Gary. But that was nothing compared to how angry he was at the person who *really* pulled the cord out of the wall.

"I can't see you, Max. But I know you're here," Jeffrey said.

"Like, I can't be. I don't have an invitation," said Max's voice close to Jeffrey's ear.

"Get lost, Max," Jeffrey said quietly.

"Can't do that, Daddy-o," Max whispered back. "The screaming's just about to start. I left a little surprise for the birthday girl in her tree house."

"Screaming? Max, what are you talking about?" Jeffrey said.

"I'm not talking about anything," Max said with a laugh. "I'm not here, remember?"

"Look at this! Look what I found in the tree house," Melissa said angrily. She hurried down the ladder carrying a long green snake that wrapped itself around her arm. "Only a dink like Gary thinks a snake would frighten a girl!"

Jeffrey laughed. "Yeah—he must think this is still the 1950s!"

Max appeared sitting in the oak tree. "Ha, ha," he said. "Like, it's so funny I forgot to laugh."

"I'm going to put this snake in Gary's pillowcase," Melissa said. "He deserves it. He's going to try to ruin my party. I know he is."

"Wait, Melissa," Jeffrey said, taking the snake from her. "It's not fair to the snake. Besides, Gary won't ruin your party."

"How do you know?"

How do I know? Jeffrey thought to himself. I know because I know who will try to ruin your party. Max! But Jeffrey couldn't tell Melissa that. She didn't even believe Max existed!

"Just take my word for it," Jeffrey said. "I can handle Gary."

"No offense, Jeffrey, but you're not in Gary's league. He's a major-league creep," Melissa said.

"Just the same, I *promise* you Gary won't ruin the party," Jeffrey said. But he thought to himself, Too bad I can't say the same thing about Max!

# Chapter Eight

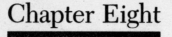

In no time at all it was Saturday, the day of Melissa's birthday. The party started at two o'clock. Kenny Thompsen was the first person to arrive. However, he arrived at *Jeffrey's* house, not at Melissa's. He was too shy to go over to Melissa's house alone.

Jeffrey was in his room wrapping his present for Melissa when Kenny rang the doorbell. Max was sitting on Jeffrey's bed. They were having an argument—the same one they had had all week.

"Max, you can't go to the party," Jeffrey said.

"Says you and whose army?" Max said. "Like, I dig surprise parties. They're a gas."

"Max, this isn't a surprise party," Jeffrey said.

Max smiled. "Sure it is. You just aren't hip to all the surprises I've got planned." He disappeared when Kenny walked into the room.

"Hi, Jeffrey," Kenny said. "What'd you get Melissa?"

"Batter's helmet with a built-in L.E.D. scoreboard," Jeffrey said. "What about you?"

"Two books by Robert Louis Stevenson," Kenny said.

"But, Kenny, *you're* the one who loves to read. Not Melissa," Jeffrey said.

"Yeah. Lucky for me, Melissa's great about lending her books," Kenny said. "Let's go."

They walked next door to Melissa's house. Melissa had her hair braided and tied with bright satin ribbons for the party. She greeted everyone at the door and told them to go into the backyard.

Outside, music was blaring. The boys were eating all the snacks and the girls were dancing. Everyone was having a great time.

But Jeffrey just couldn't relax and enjoy it. He was too busy looking for the uninvited guest—or rather, the uninvited ghost!

"Hey, Kenny," Melissa said. "Becky Singer is looking for you."

"Why?" Kenny asked. Kenny seemed to be the only person in the world who didn't get it that Becky Singer liked him.

"Maybe she wants to borrow a book," Jeffrey teased. He went over to the snack table where Benjamin Hyde was trying one of everything.

"You know what I don't like about parties, Jeffrey?" Ben said. "They make too much garbage."

"Ben, you're getting nuts about garbage," Jeffrey said.

"Look at this," Ben said. "Paper plates and paper napkins. Soda cans. Plastic spoons. Paper hats. And after the party, someone's going to have to make it all disappear!"

Speaking of disappearing, Jeffrey wondered where Max was. He had threatened to show up at the party, but so far he was a no-show. Of course, Max could be there and still be a no-show, Jeffrey realized.

Suddenly, there were two screams at the table with the punch bowl. Mandy Lutrell and her twin sister Mindy were standing there with identical purple stains on their identical pink dresses. "There are holes in the bottoms of the paper cups!" Mandy yelled.

"Fruit punch dripped all over our dresses," Mindy said.

Melissa came rushing over. "I'm really sorry, you guys. Come on in the house and we'll wash it."

"Hey, Melissa, there are holes in *all* of these cups," Kenny said.

"Oh, no." Ben moaned. "They'll all have to be thrown out."

A little spilled fruit punch wasn't the worst tragedy in the world. But everyone knew how much Mindy and Mandy Lutrell cared about looking nice. So everyone was very sympathetic—except for Gary.

"Crybabies," Gary said, laughing.

Melissa had had enough. "Gary, get out of here," she said. "Mom told you to stay away from my party."

"Oh, go get your girlfriends a bib," Gary said, turning his back on Melissa and walking into the house. But a few minutes later he was back outside, stuffing potato chips into his mouth.

"Hey! Let's hit the piñata!" Jeffrey said. He was trying to get everyone's attention back on the party.

Kenny went first. He put on the blindfold and swung at the piñata. But it didn't break. Then it was Ben's turn.

Ben swung and hit the piñata straight-on. Suddenly, water sprayed out all over the place, soaking Kenny and Ben. Gary laughed so hard he had to hold his stomach.

"Someone filled the piñata with water balloons," Kenny said, looking very wet.

Melissa's party was falling apart.

Just then, the music that was blaring out of the speakers changed. Instead of Melissa's Michael Jackson and U-2 records, it was 1950s rock 'n' roll.

Melissa rushed over to her brother. "I hate you and I'll never forgive you," she said. Gary just laughed.

Jeffrey didn't think it was possible, but he actually felt sorry for Gary. Melissa was blaming him, and Jeffrey knew the trouble wasn't Gary's fault. The 1950s music said it all. It was Max. It had to be Max. Max, who *used* to be Jeffrey's friend.

Jeffrey wanted to strangle Max, but he'd have to find him first.

"Listen, everybody," Melissa announced from the back steps. "Let's just go downstairs for cake and ice cream. And I'll open my presents."

Everyone except Jeffrey walked into the house. He stayed behind and called out, "Max, wherever you are, you're in deep trouble."

Max appeared, drinking a soda. He looked so real that it was hard for Jeffrey to believe no one else could see him.

"Soda in cans—what a groove," Max said. "Next thing, we may even put a man on the moon."

"How about a ghost on the moon?" Jeffrey said angrily.

But before Jeffrey could say anything else, he heard Melissa shout from inside the house.

"Oh, no!" she cried.

Jeffrey went running to see what Max had done now.

"The cake! All my presents! They're gone!" Melissa shouted. "I knew he'd do it! I knew Gary would ruin my party!"

Jeffrey pushed his way into the room. The long Ping-Pong table, which had been covered with birthday presents and cake, was clean and empty. Everything, including the decorations, was gone.

Melissa looked at Gary, who stood off in the corner with a smile. Then she looked at Jeffrey.

"I thought you said you could handle him!" she yelled as she ran out of the room in tears.

# Chapter Nine

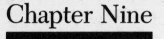

How could Max do it? Jeffrey wondered. How could he take Melissa's cake and presents away? This was going too far—even for a ghost!

None of Melissa's friends knew what to say. They had never seen Melissa cry before. A minute later, they heard her slam her door at the top of the stairs. The echo seemed to make the whole house shake.

Finally, Becky Singer, Melissa's best friend, said, "I'm going to go tell Melissa's mom."

"Maybe her parents will put Gary up for adoption," Ben said.

Everyone thought Gary had stolen the presents and the cake. Jeffrey felt worse than ever, knowing it was really his friend Max.

Finally, Melissa's mother called down the stairs. She asked everyone to go wait in the backyard for a while.

But as Jeffrey started to go outside, he felt

someone tap him on the shoulder. He turned around. No one was there. No one he could see.

"Okay, I know you're here, Max," Jeffrey said. "Where are you?"

"Hey, Daddy-o," Max said as he materialized. Max was sitting on the Ping-Pong table wearing one of the birthday-party hats. "Listen . . ."

But Jeffrey wanted to do the talking, not the listening.

"Where are Melissa's presents?" he asked.

"Search me, Daddy-o."

"Come on, Max. How could you do this?"

"Like, I was just trying to be the life of this party," Max said.

"Funny thing for a ghost to say," Jeffrey said.

"Hey, I used to go to every birthday party in my school. And, like, I was so much fun to be with, sometimes cats I didn't even know at other schools invited me to their parties. I was the *king*!" Max said. He looked away from Jeffrey sadly. "I don't make the scene at parties anymore. I haven't even blown out a birthday candle of my own in thirty years."

"I'm sorry about that, Max. I really am," Jeffrey said. "But you shouldn't have taken Melissa's presents."

"I'm hip. That's why I didn't do the deed," Max said.

"What? You mean you didn't take them?" Jeffrey asked.

"No, Daddy-o. It's not cool to make girls cry—at least not when it's their party. But I know who did it."

"Let me guess. Does his name begin with a G and end with slimeball?" Jeffrey said, thinking immediately of Melissa's brother, Gary.

"That's the cat. Grade-A, one-hundred-percent fink," Max said. "And I could dig spoiling his afternoon."

Jeffrey started lacing his sneakers tighter. He always did that when he was getting an idea. "Hey, would you really like to help me?" Jeffrey asked. "I've got to get Melissa's presents back."

"The most, Daddy-o."

Jeffrey assumed that meant yes. "Okay, Max, you can. Come on. I've got a great idea," he said, hurrying upstairs.

Jeffrey found Gary watching TV in the living room. He snapped off the TV to get Gary's attention. But then he started to think for a minute—did he really want to go through with his plan? Gary was two years older than he was. And Gary was big for his age. And pounding Melissa's friends was Gary's second-most favorite thing to do. (Pounding Melissa was the first.)

Gary glared at Jeffrey. "What is it, turkey?"

"Gary, I've got to show you something," Jeffrey said. "You're not going to believe it."

Gary looked at Jeffrey as though he didn't believe it already. "What?" he said.

"It's in the laundry room," Jeffrey said. "Come on."

The three of them crowded into the small laundry room. There wasn't much room next to the washer and dryer and ironing board.

"Well?" Gary asked after he closed the door behind him.

Jeffrey took a deep breath and asked, "What did you do with Melissa's presents?"

Gary gave Jeffrey a shove and went for the door. But it wouldn't open.

"Hey, the door's locked," Gary said.

Jeffrey almost said, "I know—Max locked it." But he didn't. "I know. *I* locked it," Jeffrey said.

"Huh?" Gary asked. Which was his way of asking a question.

"Yes, I locked it—with my mind," Jeffrey said. "Have I ever told you about my mental powers?"

"What mental powers?" Gary scoffed. "I'd need a magnifying glass to see your brain."

"Gary, for your own good, don't force me to use my mental powers on you," Jeffrey said. "I can hurt you without lifting a finger."

"Just looking at you hurts, slimeball."

"Gary, if you don't tell me where Melissa's presents are right now, I'm going to *think* about hurting you."

Gary laughed.

"You don't believe me, do you?" Jeffrey asked.

"No way," Gary said.

Jeffrey closed his eyes. In a faraway voice he said, "I'm thinking about stomping on your right foot." Then he winked at Max, who was standing right next to Gary—although Gary couldn't see him.

Max got the signal loud and clear. And with a big grin on his face, he jumped on Gary's right foot.

"Yeeeow!" Gary yelled. His eyes went wide with surprise. "How did you do that?"

"With my mind," Jeffrey said. "Now, I'll give you one more chance. Where are Melissa's presents?"

"If you're such a brain, why don't you read *my* mind!" Gary snapped.

Jeffrey closed his eyes again. "Okay. You asked for it. I'm thinking about making you sit down, Gary," he said.

Max wasn't sure what Jeffrey had in mind. So

he just jumped on both of Gary's feet at the same time and pushed hard against Gary's chest. Gary sat down real fast.

"Okay, okay!" Gary cried. "The stupid presents are in the basement. I hid them in an old trunk." He looked at Jeffrey suspiciously. "How did you do that?"

"I have friends in places where you don't even know there are places," Jeffrey said, winking at Max.

"Huh?" Gary asked.

It didn't take very long for the party to get rolling again after that. With Jeffrey's help, the presents were found and the cake was discovered. And Melissa was perfectly happy again.

"Make a wish and blow out the candles," Mrs. McKane said. She lit the candles on Melissa's cake.

It was a tough choice for Melissa and the candles were burning quickly. Should she wish to be the first girl on a major league baseball team? Should she wish that she would always have friends like Becky, Jeffrey, Ben, and Kenny? Or should she just wish her brother would fall into a hole somewhere?

Friends it was! She took a deep breath and started blowing the candles out one by one. One— two—three—four . . . Suddenly, Melissa could tell she was going to run out of air before all the candles were out. And then she wouldn't get her wish.

Everyone was cheering her on. But only Jeffrey saw what happened next. A transparent boy in a 1950s plaid shirt leaned in close to Melissa's face. And then Max blew, giving the candles a blast that almost sent them flying off the cake.

"Hey, can you dig that?" Max said, looking at Jeffrey. "Still the king after all these years."

Later that night, just before Jeffrey's bedtime, Jeffrey and Max were talking. Jeffrey was lying on his bed and Max was leaning back in Jeffrey's desk chair.

"Thanks for helping me out today, and Melissa, too," Jeffrey said. "The party would have been a disaster without you."

They were both chewing bubble gum from the party bag Jeffrey had brought home.

"Like, your friends are my friends," Max said.

"Then why can't they see you?" Jeffrey said.

"I'm working on that, Daddy-o. I'm working on that," Max said. "Well, toss you now and catch you later."

Jeffrey knew that meant Max was getting ready to leave.

"Where are you going?" Jeffrey asked.

Max stuck his bubble gum on Jeffrey's desk. "Save it for me," he said. "I'll be back."

"Why don't you ever answer my questions?"

"See you later, alligator," Max said, beginning to fade out.

"After a while, crocodile," Jeffrey answered.

Hearing Jeffrey say something from the 1950s made Max laugh. "Hey, you're speaking my lingo!" he said. "That's totally awesome!" And then he was gone.

"Totally awesome?" Jeffrey said with surprise. He grinned and turned out the light. "I *knew* he'd learn fast."

**Here's a peek at Jeffrey's next adventure with Max, the third-grade ghost!**

## HAUNTED HALLOWEEN

Jeffrey looked up from his homework and there was Max sitting on his window sill.

"What took you so long in the old McGyver house today, Max?" Jeffrey asked. "Is it really haunted? Did you see any ghosts?"

"Nope," Max answered. "No ghosts. And I thought it would be cool to run into one, too."

"Well," Jeffrey said, "if there was nothing in the McGyver house, what took you so long in there?"

Max started walking through the air on his hands. "Oh, I don't know. I was checking it out, that's all. And I'm telling you, the McGyver house was dullsville—except for one thing."

"What?"

"A knife."

"A knife?" Jeffrey cried.

"Did I say knife?" said Max with a sly smile. "I meant a *dagger.*"

"A dagger!" Jeffrey echoed.

"Like, it's about this big," Max said, showing Jeffrey with his hands. Sometimes it looked like the dagger was six inches long and sometimes it looked three feet long. "Oops!" Max said suddenly. "Time for me to make like the wind and blow. Plant you now and dig you later, Jeffrey."

"Wait, Max!" Jeffrey said. "What about the dagger?" But a moment later, Jeffrey was alone in his room, talking to himself. And Max was gonesville.

## ABOUT THE AUTHORS

Bill and Megan Stine have written numerous books for young readers, including titles in these series: *The Cranberry Cousins; Wizards, Warriors, and You; The Three Investigators; Indiana Jones; G.I. Joe;* and *Jem.* They live on New York City's Upper West Side with their seven-year-old son, Cody, who believes in ghosts.